This book belongs to

....

To my husband's children, Karimi, Ciku, Mwangi & Wajii, all my love.
Wanuri

To my supportive and loving sister, Sara.
Manuela

First published in the United Kingdom in 2017 by
Lantana Publishing Ltd., London.

Text © Wanuri Kahiu 2017
Illustration © Manuela Adreani 2017

ISBN-13: 978-1-911373-13-1

A CIP catalogue record for this book is available from the British Library.
Printed in the EU.

This book can be ordered directly from the publishers from the website:
www.lantanapublishing.com

The Wooden Camel

WRITTEN BY

Wanuri Kahiu

ILLUSTRATED BY

Manuela Adreani

LANTANA PUBLISHING

Etabo dreams about racing camels.
He thinks it will feel like flying.

He knows he will surely beat his older
brother Lopeyok when they race.

All his brothers and sisters make fun of Etabo. He's too small to race camels.

But Etabo doesn't care. He knows he will be the best camel racer ever.

One day, their father tells them they have to sell all the camels for money to buy water.

Etabo is upset and wonders if he will ever have the chance to race.

When Etabo asks Akuj the
Sky God for help, Akuj says:

"Your dreams are enough."

With no camels to mind, Etabo and his sister Akiru
and brother Lopeyok are sent to look after the goats.

It is a boring chore but Keti, their favourite goat, keeps them amused.

Keti likes to shake his head and blow raspberries at them. Sometimes he even head-butts Etabo's bottom.

But the cost of water is rising and Etabo's
older siblings have to find work.

Etabo is left to look after the goats alone,
with only Keti to keep him company.

Etabo sits in a small acacia tree daydreaming about racing camels. In his dreams he can fly, somersault and even catapult himself onto soft sand dunes.

But his dreams are not enough.

When Etabo goes to see his
sister Akiru at work, she lets him
pat the horses she looks after.

One nuzzles his hand and licks
his face.

"Yuuuuuuuckkk!" Etabo
screeches.

Although Etabo knows it's against the rules, he begs Akiru to let him ride the horses, but she won't agree.

So instead, Etabo tries to ride...

Chickens...

Cats...

And even Keti...

But none of them will have it.

He prays to Akuj again,
and again Akuj whispers:

"Your dreams are enough."

Akiru watches her brother becoming more and
more unhappy and decides to make him a gift.

So she whittles and whittles, and makes Etabo
his very own herd of wooden camels.

"Now you can race the wind," Akiru says.

Etabo rushes to the sandy hill with Keti to play
with his wooden camels.

As he races them, he sings to them and they seem
to come to life, right there before his eyes...

That night, before bed, Etabo hugs his
sister and thanks her for her kind gift.
He remembers Akuj's words.

His dreams are enough!

Etabo falls asleep clutching his new best friends.

He drops into a deep dream world where he races his wooden camels and wins the camel derby.